Sister Night & Sister Day

told & illustrated by BETH NORLING

ALLEN & UNWIN

For mum and dad, thankyou for teaching me the love and language of drawing and for your endless support and encouragement

Special thankyou to Sue Flockhart
Tegan and Joss Bennett ~
without your words there
would be no story to tell...

Ruby and Rose were twins. They looked alike,
but in their hearts they were as different as night and day.
Ruby was kind and hardworking, while Rose thought of
no one but herself and was always quick
with an excuse not to help.
In their mother's eyes,
however, Rose could do
no wrong, for Rose was
her golden girl.

So while Rose played, Ruby sat alone by the well
spinning mountains of fleece into thread.

One afternoon while she was spinning, Ruby pricked herself on the spindle and her finger began to bleed. She went to wash the blood from the spindle but it slipped out of her hand and sank to the bottom of the well.

Ruby ran to her mother in tears, but her mother had no kind words. She was angry and sent Ruby away, shouting, 'Don't come back until you have found my spindle!'

DON'T COME BACK UNTIL...

Crying, Ruby ran back to look
for the spindle, but the well
was too deep and too dark.
'It's lost,' whispered Ruby,
her tears falling one by one
into the cold water below.
With a sigh she climbed to
the edge of the well and
threw herself in. Sinking
softly, slowly, she slipped
into a dream.

Ruby woke in a shining meadow. Through the grass ran a path and she followed it till she came to an enormous brick oven. From inside the oven voices cried,

'Oh, take us out! Take us out or we shall burn. We have been baked a long, long time!' Ruby opened the door. The oven was filled with loaves of baking hot bread.

OH, TAKE US OUT!

The heat from within
scorched Ruby's pretty face.
All the same, she took out the loaves
one by one, till it was done,
then went on her way.

An old apple tree stood with its branches hanging over the path. 'Shake me! Oh, shake me or my boughs will break!' cried the tree, 'for my apples are heavy and ripe!'

Ruby shook the tree
till the apples fell like rain, and gathered
them together, every last one, then went on her way.

It was dark when she came to a strange little house
and tiptoed to the window. Inside sat a woman unlike any Ruby
had ever seen. She wore a coat of night and a dress of day,
which filled the room with sunbeams and moonlight.

'Don't be afraid,' the woman said.
'You are here to learn the work of my house.
But take care, for what is done inside my house
will also be done upon the earth.'
'Who are you?' asked Ruby in a small voice.

So Ruby went to work.
She collected wood for the fire,
potatoes from the fields and
water from the well.

She opened the doors
and windows of the little
house to let the sweet wind
blow through.

Day by day a gladness
filled her heart till
she was brimming
with it.

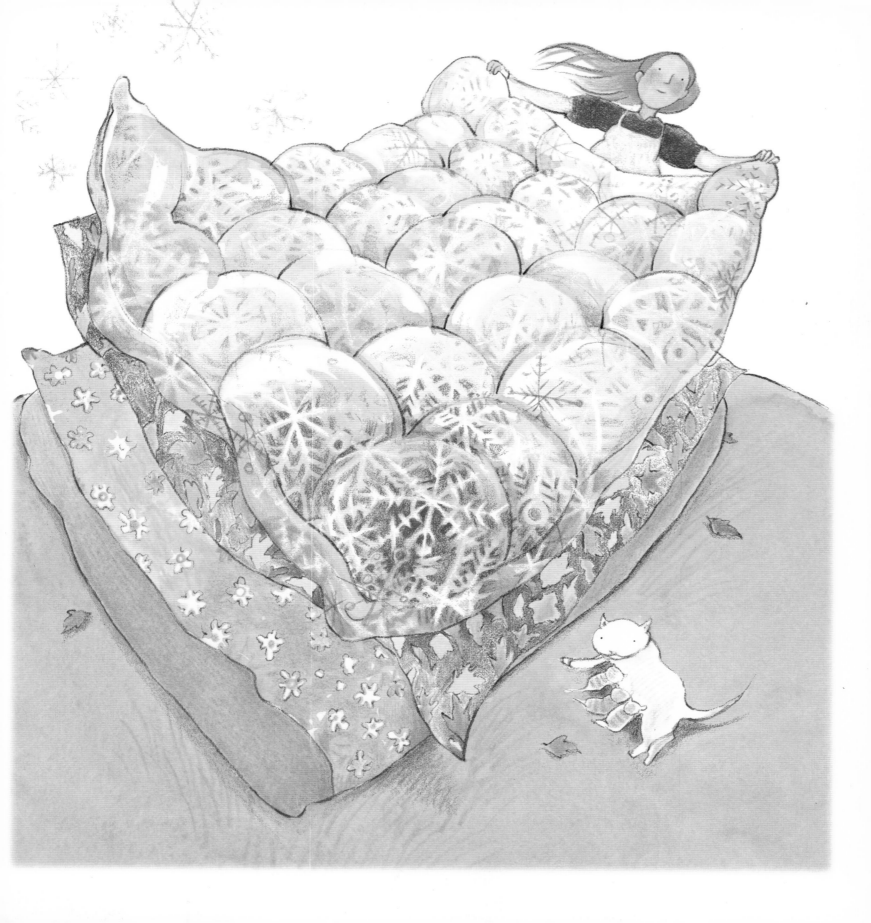

All that Ruby did was good,
and Mother Earth saw that it was so.

On the earth the seasons were mild, days were long and warm,
there was plenty to eat and everyone was content.

AND EVERYONE WAS CONTENT

Then one morning Ruby
began to think of home.
'I have been happy here,'
she said to Mother Earth,
'but now I must go back
to be with my sister Rose.'

Mother Earth led Ruby to her door. As Ruby stood on the threshold, thread upon glittering thread fell around her until she was covered in a golden cloth that shone like the sun.

Mother Earth said,
'All is as it should be.'

ALL IS AS IT SHOULD BE

COCK-A-DOODLE-DOO!

The door closed and Ruby found herself by the well
at her mother's house. The rooster crowed,
'Cock-a-doodle-doo! Your golden girl's come back to you.'

Seeing Ruby's golden dress,
Mother and Rose hurried to greet her.
'Where did you find this glorious
cloth?' said Mother. 'My Rose
must have some too.'

At once Rose was sent to the well,

but she was too lazy to spin.

She pricked her finger on a thorn so that it bled...

tossed the spindle into the well,
and jumped in after it.

Rose woke in the shining meadow, and followed the very same
path that Ruby had trod. As she passed the oven the bread cried,
'Oh, take us out, take us out or we shall burn.
We have been baked a long, long time!'

But the lazy girl replied,
'Burn if you like. I'm not about to
make myself dirty and hot!'

Rose came next to the old apple tree
and it cried out again, 'Oh, shake me, shake me
or my boughs will break. My apples are heavy and ripe!'

The lazy girl replied, 'Break if you like.
I won't have apples fall on my pretty head!'

It was still day when she came
to the strange little house.

'Such a small house will
be easy to keep,' she said to
herself. And she marched
in to tell Mother Earth
she had come.

On the first day Rose worked hard, thinking of all the gold that would soon be hers. On the second day she did half as much work, and on the third day half as much again... until...the day came when she didn't bother to get out of bed at all.

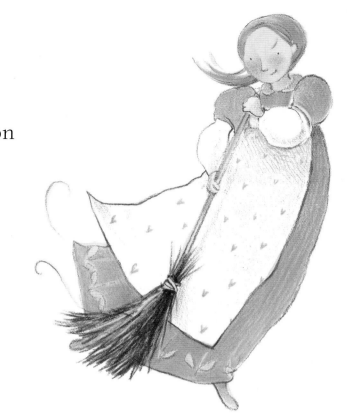

Snow fell on the earth and did not thaw in time for spring. Days were bitterly cold and the nights seemed as if they would last for ever. Nothing would grow and people went hungry.

Snow fell upon the earth and did not thaw... Days were bitterly cold. Nothing would grow and people went hungry...

Mother Earth could bear it no longer and told the girl that she must go. Rose was eager to leave, and thought, 'Now I'll be covered in gold!'

NOW LEAVE!

gold

Mother Earth led her to the same door and Rose waited on the threshold. But it was not gold that fell. A shower of thistles and thorns rained down upon her until she was all but covered in prickles. Mother Earth spoke firmly as she shut the door.
'All is as it should be.'

ALL IS AS IT SHOULD BE

Rose soon found herself back by the well at her mother's house.
The rooster crowed when he saw her, 'Cock-a-doodle-doo!
Your thorny girl's come back to you!'

COCK-A-DOODLE-DOO!

Mother was too shocked to speak.

But Ruby was glad to see her sister again and said,

'Rose, come in and help me bake some bread.'

Rose paused for a moment.

'Maybe I will,' she said.

First published in 2000

Allen & Unwin
9 Atchison Street
St Leonards NSW 2065
Australia
Phone: (61 2) 8425 0100
Fax: (61 2) 9906 2218
Email: frontdesk@allen-unwin.com.au
Web: http://www.allen-unwin.com.au

Sister Night & Sister Day is a retelling of the Grimm's fairy tale 'Mother Holle', from *The Complete Grimm's Fairy Tales* by
J.L.K. and W.K. Grimm, trans. by Margaret Hunt & James Stern.
The Complete Grimm's Fairy Tales is copyright © 1944 by Pantheon Books. Copyright renewed 1972 by Random House, Inc.
Adaption based on 'Mother Holle' reprinted by permission of Pantheon Books,
a division of Random House, Inc.

National Library of Australia
Cataloguing-in-Publication entry:

Norling, Beth.
Sister night and sister day.

ISBN 1 86448 863 8 (hb).
ISBN 1 86448 819 0 (pb).

Title.

A823.3

Beth Norling designed and illustrated this book
using watercolour pencil, watercolour and conté pencil

Designed and typeset by Sandra Nobes
Set in 16pt Veljovic
Printed in China by Everbest Printing Co. Ltd.

1 3 5 7 9 10 8 6 4 2